Ms. Raccoon
Night
School

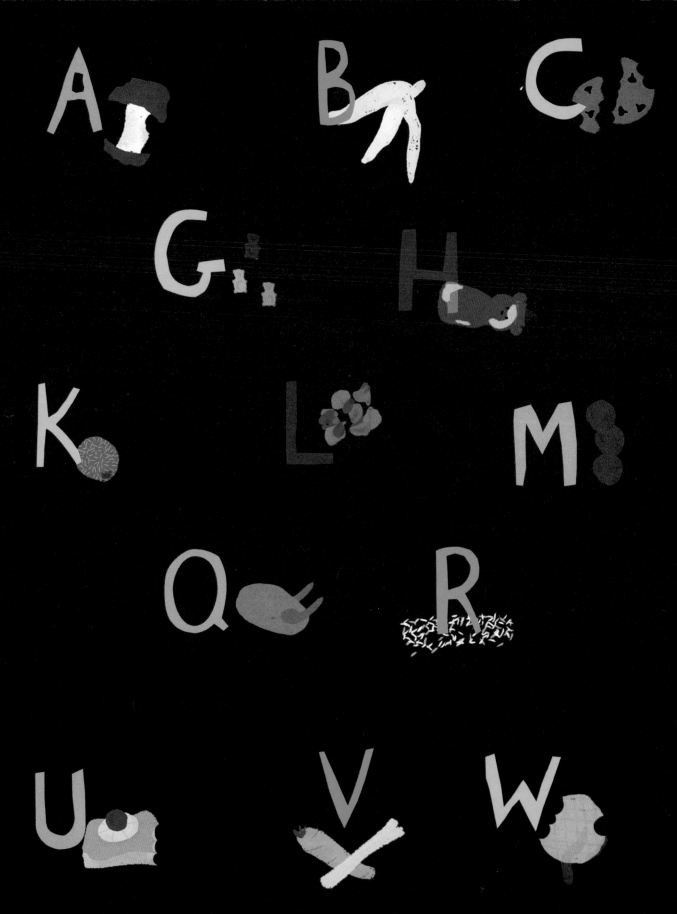

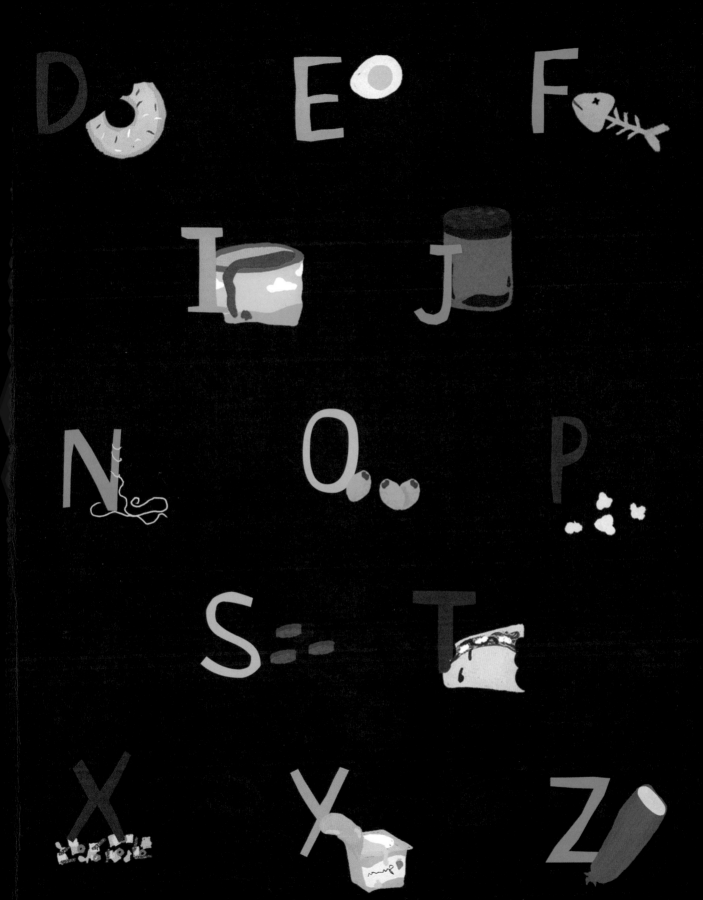

Late at night, stars fill the sky.
The air feels cool.
Ms. Raccoon prepares her classroom
for the night school.

The trash can lid clanks
and all the kits grab a seat.
They'll learn great, new lessons
and find something to eat.

Into the gray trash can,
Ms. Raccoon dives down deep.
Bags, wrappers and
containers create a big heap.

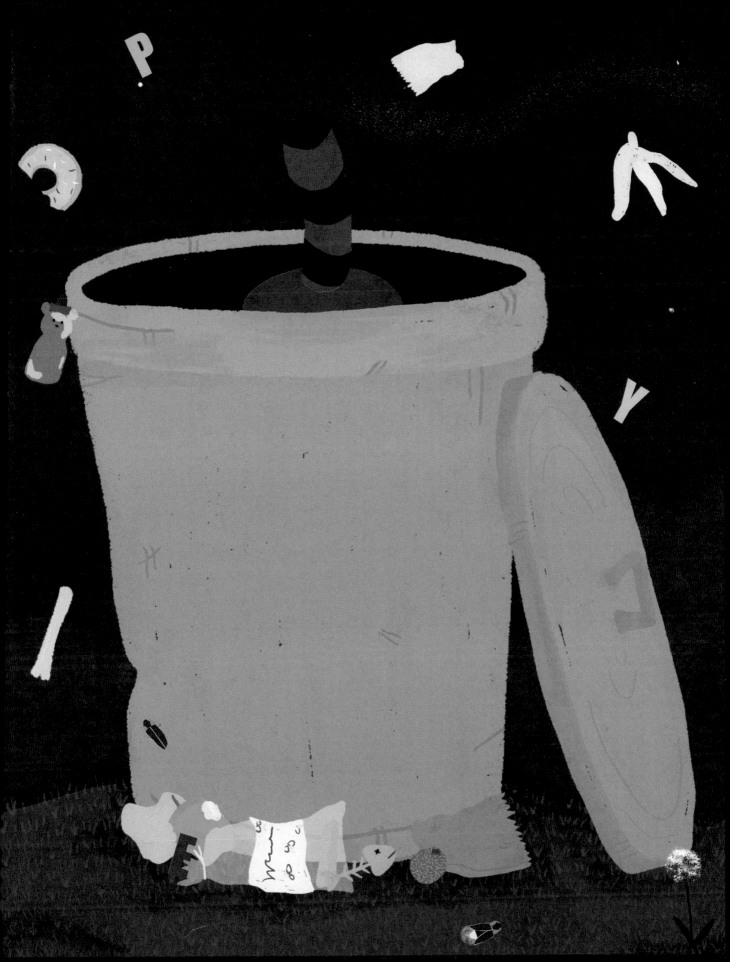

Ms. Raccoon pulls out
twenty six delicious bits
in order to teach
her three, lovely, little kits.

"Tonight, my students, you will learn
an important set -
the letters and sounds
that we call the alphabet."

A is for Apple

B is for Banana

C is for Cookie

D is for Donut

E is for Egg

F is for Fish

G is for Gummy bears

H is for Honey

I is for Ice cream

J is for Jelly
K is for Kiwi

L is for Lettuce

M is for Meatballs
N is for Noodles

O is for Olive

P is for Popcorn

Q is for Quail

R is for Rice

S is for Sausage

T is for Taco

U is for Upside down cake

V is for Veggies

W is for Waffle

X is in snack miX

Y is for Yogurt

Z is for Zucchini

The teacher and students
nibble, bite, chew and chomp.
Then the kits get to enjoy
a quick recess romp.

They have learned letters and sounds -
things that are brand new.
At night's end, they have full bellies -
and full minds, too.

Made in the USA
Monee, IL
23 February 2021